Días y días
Days and Days

BY ✳ POR
Ginger Foglesong Guy

ILLUSTRATIONS BY ✳ ILUSTRACIONES DE
René King Moreno

Greenwillow Books, *An Imprint of* HarperCollins *Publishers*

Cowsie Cow jumped into bed.

"Good night," said Cowsie Cow.
"Good night," said Moosie Moose.
"Good night," said Bearsie Bear.

Cowsie Cow, Moosie Moose, and Bearsie Bear
were just falling asleep.
Suddenly there was tapping at the door.
"Here we go again," said Moosie Moose.
"Who is it?" said Bearsie Bear.

"It's me, Piggie Pig," said Piggie Pig.

"Piggie Pig?" said Cowsie Cow.
"Piggie Pig?" said Moosie Moose.
"Piggie Pig?" said Bearsie Bear.
"Yes, Piggie Pig," said Piggie Pig.

"I'll take care of this," said Cowsie Cow.
So Cowsie Cow opened the door and said,
"Piggie Pig, it's cold outside, and you want to sleep over."
"I was about to say that," said Piggie Pig.
"I know," said Cowsie Cow.
"What shall we do about Piggie Pig?"
said Cowsie Cow.

Just then the wind screeched and squealed.
"Please?" said Piggie Pig.
"Piggie Pig may sleep over,"
said Bearsie Bear.
"Hooray!" said Piggie Pig.

Piggie Pig jumped into bed.

"Good night," said Piggie Pig.
"Good night," said Cowsie Cow.
"Good night," said Moosie Moose.
"Good night," said Bearsie Bear.

Piggie Pig, Cowsie Cow, Moosie Moose,
and Bearsie Bear were just falling asleep.
Suddenly there was scratching at the door.
"This is going to be a long night," said Cowsie Cow.
"You can say that again," said Moosie Moose.
"This is going to be a long night," Cowsie Cow said it again.
"Who is it?" said Bearsie Bear.

"It's me, Foxie Fox," said Foxie Fox.

"Foxie Fox?" said Piggie Pig.
"Foxie Fox?" said Cowsie Cow.
"Foxie Fox?" said Moosie Moose.
"Foxie Fox?" said Bearsie Bear.
"Yes, Foxie Fox," said Foxie Fox.

"I'll get it," said Piggie Pig.
So Piggie Pig opened the door and said,
"Foxie Fox, it's cold outside, and you want to sleep over."
"I was about to say that," said Foxie Fox.
"I know," said Piggie Pig.
"What shall we do about Foxie Fox?"
said Piggie Pig.

Just then the wind growled and howled.
"Please?" said Foxie Fox.
"Foxie Fox may sleep over," said Bearsie Bear.
"Hooray!" said Foxie Fox.

Foxie Fox jumped into bed.

"Good night," said Foxie Fox.
"Good night," said Piggie Pig.
"Good night," said Cowsie Cow.
"Good night," said Moosie Moose.
"Good night," said Bearsie Bear.

"Somebody here has cold hooves,"
said Moosie Moose.
"Well, don't look at me," said Cowsie Cow.

Foxie Fox, Piggie Pig, Cowsie Cow,
Moosic Moose, and Bearsie Bear
were just falling asleep.
Suddenly there was scratching at the door.
"Who is it?" said Bearsie Bear.

"It's me, Goosie Goose," said Goosie Goose.

"Goosie Goose?" said Foxie Fox.
"Goosie Goose?" said Piggie Pig.
"Goosie Goose?" said Cowsie Cow.
"Goosie Goose?" said Moosie Moose.
"Goosie Goose?" said Bearsie Bear.
"Yes, Goosie Goose," said Goosie Goose.

"Allow me," said Foxie Fox.
So Foxie Fox opened the door and said,
"Goosie Goose, it's cold outside, and you want to sleep over."
"I was about to say that," said Goosie Goose.
"I know," said Foxie Fox.
"What shall we do about Goosie Goose?"
said Foxie Fox.

Just then the wind blasted and blustered.
"Please?" said Goosie Goose.
"Goosie Goose may sleep over,"
said Bearsie Bear.
"Hooray!" said Goosie Goose.

Goosie Goose jumped into bed.

"Good night," said Goosie Goose.
"Good night," said Foxie Fox.
"Good night," said Piggie Pig.
"Good night," said Cowsie Cow.
"Good night," said Moosie Moose.
"Good night," said Bearsie Bear.

Goosie Goose, Foxie Fox, Piggie Pig,
Cowsie Cow, Moosie Moose, and Bearsie Bear
were just falling asleep.
Suddenly there was scratching at the door.
"I'll say, Who is it?" said Piggie Pig.
"Who is it?" said Piggie Pig.

"It's me, Porkie Porcupine,"
said Porkie Porcupine.

"Uh-oh," said Goosie Goose.
"Uh-oh," said Foxie Fox.
"Uh-oh," said Piggie Pig.
"Uh-oh," said Cowsie Cow.
"Uh-oh," said Moosie Moose.
"Uh-oh," said Bearsie Bear.

"What shall we do about Porkie Porcupine?"
everyone asked.
Just then the wind rumbled and grumbled.

"I'll get it," said Bearsie Bear.
So Bearsie Bear opened the door,
and before he could say a word,
Porkie Porcupine peeked in and exclaimed,
"Ooooooh! A PARTY!
A GREAT BIG SLEEPOVER PARTY!"

Porkie Porcupine jumped into bed.

"Ouch!" said Goosie Goose.
"Ouch!" said Foxie Fox.
"Ouch!" said Piggie Pig.
"Ouch!" said Cowsie Cow.
"Ouch!" said Moosie Moose.

"Goodbye!" said Goosie Goose.
"Goodbye!" said Foxie Fox.
"Goodbye!" said Piggie Pig.
"Goodbye!" said Cowsie Cow.
"Goodbye!" said Moosie Moose.

"Porkie Porcupine, we'll have no more of that,"
said Bearsie Bear. "If you wish to stay,
you must sleep by yourself."
Porkie Porcupine found a warm spot
under the bed.

Bearsie Bear yawned and was about
to climb into bed
when whom do you suppose he saw
peering through the window?

Goosie Goose, Foxie Fox, Piggie Pig,
Cowsie Cow, and Moosie Moose.

So Bearsie Bear opened the door and said,
"It's still cold outside, and you want
to come in again."
"We were about to say that," they answered.
"I know," said Bearsie Bear.

Just then the wind whistled and bristled.
"Please?" they said.
"You may come in again," said Bearsie Bear.
"Hooray!" said Goosie Goose, Foxie Fox,
Piggie Pig, Cowsie Cow, and Moosie Moose.

Goosie Goose, Foxie Fox, Piggie Pig, Cowsie Cow,
and Moosie Moose jumped into bed.

"Good night," said Goosie Goose.
"Good night," said Foxie Fox.
"Good night," said Piggie Pig.
"Good night," said Cowsie Cow.
"Good night," said Moosie Moose.
"Good night," said Bearsie Bear.

"Good night," said Porkie Porcupine
from under the bed. "I miss you."

"What?" said Goosie Goose.
"What?" said Foxie Fox.
"What?" said Piggie Pig.
"What?" said Cowsie Cow.
"What?" said Moosie Moose.
"What?" said Bearsie Bear.

"I miss you,"
Porkie Porcupine said it again.

Everyone was silent.
But then, after a little while, Bearsie Bear said,
"Porkie Porcupine, if you are very careful about it,
and if you are very careful not to thrash about,
you may come back to bed."
"Hooray!" said Porkie Porcupine.

So, Porkie Porcupine climbed into bed.
And he was very careful about it.
And he was very careful not to thrash about.

"Good night," said Bearsie Bear.
"Good night," said Moosie Moose.
"Good night," said Cowsie Cow.
"Good night," said Piggie Pig.
"Good night," said Foxie Fox.
"Good night," said Goosie Goose.
"Good night," said Porkie Porcupine.
"See you in the morning."

"And in the morning I'll make pancakes
for breakfast," said Bearsie Bear.
"Mmmmmm!" the others exclaimed with delight.
"Bearsie Bear has a big heart," said Moosie Moose.
"And a big, big bed," said Porkie Porcupine.
"You can say that again," said Cowsie Cow.

"And a big, big bed," Porkie Porcupine
said it again.
Everyone smiled.

And then, after another little while,
they were peacefully asleep.